A Book of Fairy Tale Bears

SELECTIONS FROM FAVORITE FOLKLORE STORIES

EDITED BY CLIFTON JOHNSON
ILLUSTRATED BY FRANK A. NANKIVELL

apocalypsewriters.com

A Book of Fairy Tale Bears:
Selections from Favorite Folklore Stories
edited by Clifton Johnson
Illustrated by Frank A. Nankivell

Published by The Writers of the Apocalypse
117 N Carbon Street, PMB 208
Marion, IL 62959

Find our books online at: http://woksprint.com

ISBN Print: 978-1-944322-54-0
Digital: 978-1-944322-92-2

Cover assembly: K. J. Joyner

A BOOK OF FAIRY-TALE BEARS

ILLUSTRATED BY

FRANK A. NANKIVELL

TABLE OF CONTENTS

The Three Bears

(PUBLISHER'S NOTE: This tale is more famously known as *Goldilocks and the Three Bears*.)

Once UPON A TIME there were three bears who lived together in a house of their own in a wood. One of them was a big bear, and one was a middle-sized bear, and the other was a little bear. They each had a bowl for their porridge—a big bowl for the big bear, a middle-sized bowl for the middle-sized bear, and a little bowl for the little bear. And they each had a chair to sit in—a big chair for the big bear, a middle-sized chair for the middle-sized bear, and a little chair for the little bear. Besides, they each had a bed to sleep in—a big bed for the big bear, a middle-sized bed for the middle-sized bear, and a little bed for the little bear.

On the borders of the wood lived a little girl named Golden Hair, and she liked to walk in the wood to pick the pretty flowers that grew there. Usually she did not go far from home after the flowers, but one warm, pleasant day she rambled on and on, picking blossoms here and there, until she was much deeper in the wood than she had ever been before.

"Now I must go back," Golden Hair said at last. "I didn't intend to come such a long way, and I'm tired and hungry."

Just then she looked on ahead up the lonely hollow into which she had wandered, and there among the trees was as nice a little house as she had ever seen.

"I didn't know that any one lived here in the wood," Golden Hair said. "I will go and find out whose house this is."

So she went to the door and rapped, but she got no response.

"Well," she said, "the people that live here can't be far away, for there is smoke coming out of the chimney. I think I will step in, if the door isn't locked."

She lifted the latch, and the door was not locked, and she went in and looked about. At one side of the room she had entered was a fireplace in which a log and some smaller sticks were smoldering. On a table were three bowls of porridge—a big bowl, and a middle-sized bowl, and a little bowl.

"The people who live in this house have set the table for dinner, I think," Golden Hair said. "If they were here I'm sure they would invite me to eat with them. Oh, how hungry I am! I wonder if they would care if I ate some of their porridge without waiting till they come. I will taste it, anyway."

So she went to the table and took a spoonful of porridge from the big bowl.

"This is too hot," she said. "I will try the next."

Then she took a spoonful of porridge from the middle-sized bowl.

"And this is too cold," she said.

Then she took a spoonful of porridge from the little bowl, and that was neither too hot nor too cold, but was just right, and she ate it all up.

"Now I must sit down to rest for a while," Golden Hair said.

Along the wall were three chairs—a big chair, a middle-sized chair, and a little chair. She tried the big chair, but it was too hard for her.

"Dear me!" Golden Hair said, "This chair won't do at all. I will try the next."

Then she sat down in the middle-sized chair, and that was too soft for her. So she tried the little chair, and that was neither too hard nor too soft, but was just right. She had settled herself in it to enjoy a good rest when **crack! Smash!** The chair broke, and Golden Hair tumbled to the floor.

"That was a nice little chair," she said as she picked herself up. "I'm sorry it is broken. How am I to rest now? I don't like the other chairs. Perhaps I had better lie down and have a nap. I must see where the beds are,"

There was another room adjoining the one in which Golden Hair had eaten the little bowl of porridge and broken the little chair. She went into it and found three beds—a big bed, and a middle-sized bed, and a little bed.

"I'm alright now," Golden Hair said; and she tried the largest bed, but it was too high at the head for her. Then she tried the middle-sized bed, and that was too high at the foot for her. Lastly she tried the little bed, and that was neither too high at the head nor too high at the foot, but was just right. She lay down on it, covered herself up, and fell fast asleep.

Meanwhile, where were the three bears? Shortly before Golden Hair rambled into the glen where they lived, they had cooked their porridge for dinner and set it on the table. Then they had gone out for a little walk to give the porridge time to cool. Golden Hair was asleep when the bears came home. As soon as they entered the kitchen and looked at the table they saw that things were not as they had left them.

"SOMEBODY HAS BEEN TASTING MY POR-RIDGE!" the big bear growled in his great gruff voice.

"And SOMEBODY HAS BEEN TASTING *MY* por-ridge!" the middle-sized bear said.

"And somebody has been tasting my porridge and eaten it all up!" the little bear piped.

"We will look around," they said, "and see if there has been any more meddling."

"SOMEBODY HAS BEEN SITTING IN MY CHAIR!" the big bear growled in his great gruff voice.

"And SOMEBODY HAS BEEN SITTING IN *MY* chair!" the middle-sized bear said.

"And somebody has been sitting in my chair and broken it all to pieces!" the little bear piped.

Then they went into their bedroom.

"SOMEBODY HAS BEEN LYING ON MY BED!" the big bear growled in his great gruff voice.

"And SOMEBODY HAS BEEN LYING ON MY bed!" the middle-sized bear said.

"And somebody has been lying on my bed, and *here she is!"* the little bear piped.

The voice of the little bear was so sharp and shrill it awakened Golden Hair at once. She sat bolt upright and stared at the three bears, and they stared at her. They were standing in a row on one side of the bed, and Golden Hair tumbled herself out at the other side before they could catch her.

Luckily the window was open, and out she leaped. Then she ran home as fast as she could go, and she never again went near the place where the three bears lived.

THE BEAR AND THE SKRATTEL

One CHRISTMAS DAY, when the king of Norway was feasting in the great hall of his palace, he proposed that a present should be sent to the King of Denmark as a pledge of his good will. "But what shall it be?" he asked.

Then spoke Anders, the king's chief huntsman. "Your Majesty," he said, "let the present be one of our handsome white bears, that the king of Denmark and his people may see the sort of creatures with which we play."

"Are you sure that a bear can be sent on so long a journey?" asked the king, "and is there any certainty that he would behave himself after he reached the Danish court?"

"Yes," Anders responded, "for I have a fellow as white as snow that I caught when he was a cub, and he will follow me wherever I go, play with my children, stand on his hind legs, and conduct himself as properly as any gentleman. I will take him to Denmark myself, if you choose."

The king was much pleased, and he ordered Anders to set off with his snow-white bear as promptly as possible.

So early the next morning Anders roused Bruin, put the king's collar round his neck, and away they went over rocks and mountains, and across valleys and plains, the nearest road to the court of the king of Denmark. It was bright weather, the sun shone, and the birds sang, and they traveled merrily on day after day till they had almost reached their journey's end. Then they came to a gloomy forest through which they tramped all one afternoon. Toward evening the wind began to whistle through the trees, and the clouds gathered and threatened a stormy night. The road, too, was very rough, and both Bruin and his master were exceedingly weary. What made matters worse was the fact that they had found no wayside inn that day, and as they had not been able to buy food they had eaten nearly all the scanty supply they carried with them.

"A pretty affair this!" Anders said. "Here I am in this lonely forest with an empty stomach, a bear for my companion, and the prospect of a wet bed."

The wind increased in violence, the clouds grew darker, and Bruin shook his ears uneasily. Anders was at his wits' end, when a woodman came whistling out of the forest, walking beside his horse, which dragged a load of fagots. The traveler stopped him and asked for a night's lodging for himself and his bear. Yet, though the woodman seemed hearty and good-natured enough, and was quite ready to provide shelter for the huntsman, he never had seen such a creature as the bear before in his life, and would have nothing to do with him on any terms.

Anders begged hard for his friend, and told how he was bringing him as a present to the king of Denmark, and how the bear was the most good-natured, best-behaved animal in the world.

The woodman, however, was not to be moved. He was sure that his wife would not like such a guest, and who could say what the bear might take it into his head to do? Moreover, their dog and their cat, their ducks and their geese would all run away for fright, whether the bear was disposed to be friendly with them or not. "No," he said in conclusion, "if you and old shaggy-back cannot part, you must spend the night in the forest, though you will have a sad time of it, no doubt."

Then he cracked his whip, clucked to his horse, and set off once more on his way homeward. The huntsman grumbled, and Bruin grunted as they resumed their plodding along the rough road. But the woodman had not gone far when he stopped his horse and again addressed Anders. "I think I can tell you a better plan than sleeping under a tree," he said. "I know where you can find shelter, if you will run the risk of getting into trouble with a mischievous skrattel who has taken up his abode in what used to be my house down the hill yonder. I lived in it until last winter, and everything had been going smoothly with us for a long time, but one unlucky night, when the storm blew as it seems likely to do tonight, that spiteful imp took it into his head to visit us. The house has ever since been in an uproar from midnight till the cock crows in the morning. Clattering footsteps run up and down the stairs and there are many other strange disturbing noises.

"What the skrattel is like no one knows. We have never seen him, nor have we seen anything belonging to him, except a queer little high-heeled shoe that he left one night in the pantry. But though we have not seen him we know he has a hand as heavy as lead, for when he chooses to thump anybody, down goes that person as if the blacksmith's hammer had hit him.

"There was no end to the goblin's monkey tricks. If the linen was hung out to dry, he cut the line. If he wanted a cup of ale he left the tap running. If the fowls were shut up he let them loose. He would drive the pig into the garden, ride on the cows, turn the horses into the hay-yard; and several times he nearly burned the house down by leaving a lighted candle among the fagots.

"He is astonishingly active and nimble. Sometimes, when he is once in motion, nothing stands still around him. Dishes and plates, pots and pans, dance about, making a dreadful sort of music, and breaking each other to pieces. The chairs and tables, too, act as if they were alive and were dancing a hornpipe or playing some wild game together.

Nor is it of any use putting things in order, for the imp would quickly turn everything upside down again.

"My wife and I bore such a lodger as long as we could, but at length we were fairly beaten; and as he seemed determined to stay permanently in the house we thought it best to give him full possession. The little rascal knew what we were about when we were preparing to move, and seemed to be in a hurry to get rid of us. So he helped us off; for on the morning we were to start, when we got up intending to load the wagon, there it was before the door with the goods on it. As we drove away we heard a loud laugh; and a sharp little voice cried out of a window, 'Good-bye, neighbors!'

"Well, he has the old house to himself now, and can play his pranks as he pleases. We have built a snug cottage for ourselves on the other side of the hill.

It is smaller and less comfortable than the old house, but we shall not go back while that skrattel is there. However, if you and your companion choose to run the hazard, you are quite welcome to the shelter; and it may be the imp is not at home tonight."

"We will try our luck," Anders said; "for anything is better than sleeping out of doors such a night as this. We may have to fight for our lodging, but never mind—Bruin will take a hand in any quarrel that arises, and the goblin will perhaps get rougher treatment from him than your house dog could give. My comrade will at any rate let the skrattel know what a bear's hug is." Then the woodman gave Anders a fagot with which to make a fire, and wished him a good night. The travelers soon found their way to the deserted house and went into the kitchen and started a fire.

"Lack-a-day!" Anders said, "I forgot one thing—I ought to have asked that good man for some supper. All I have left is a little dry bread. But I am glad we shall not be obliged to sleep in the woods. We will eat what food we have, keep ourselves warm, and get to bed as soon as we can."

So after eating all their crusts, and drinking some water from the well in the yard, the huntsman wrapped himself in his cloak, and lay down at the back of the kitchen. Bruin curled up in a corner of the wide fireplace, and both he and his master were soon sound asleep.

Midnight came. The fire was out, and everything was quiet in the house, but outside a storm was raging. Presently in popped an ugly little skrattel not much more than two feet high, with a humped back, a face like a dried pippin, and a nose like a ripe mulberry. He wore high-heeled shoes and a pointed cap. On his shoulder he carried a nice fat kid[1] skinned and ready for roasting.

"A rough night this," the goblin grumbled, "but thanks to that booby woodman I have a house to myself; and now I'll prepare a hot supper and have a glass of good ale."

He at once got busy, and soon the fire blazed up, and the kid was put on a spit, and the roasting began. When the meat was sufficiently roasted the skrattel transferred it to a covered dish, which he set in a nook of the fireplace to keep warm till he had the table ready. Next he rolled a keg of ale from the closet, drank a glass, and then, in the joy of his heart, rubbed his hands, tossed up his red cap, and danced and sang before the hearth.

Meanwhile the huntsman had waked up, and was lying very quiet looking on from the back of the room. Sometimes he quaked with fear, and sometimes he

---

[1] *Don't panic, dear readers! Most likely the author meant a young goat. - the Publisher*

licked his lips at thought of the savory supper the skrattel had prepared and was half minded to fight for its possession.

Suddenly the skrattel observed Bruin lying fast asleep rolled up like a ball in the chimney-corner. He at once went closer and looked at the bear very sharply, doubtful what he really was. "One of the family, I suppose," the skrattel said to himself.

Just then Bruin gave his ears a shake and showed a little of his snout. "Oho!" the imp exclaimed. "I see what it is. It's a mouse; but what a large one! Where could he have come from? Shall I let him alone or drive him out? Perhaps he may do me some mischief, but I am not afraid of rats and mice. I have driven away every other living thing out of the house, and this brute shall follow them without any more delay. So here goes."

The elf took up the spit he had used in roasting the kid, and brought it down with a rousing thump on the bear's head. Bruin raised himself slowly up, snorted, and shook himself. Then he walked across the room and back, and grinned at his enemy. The skrattel, somewhat alarmed, retreated a few paces, and stood with the spit in his hand prepared for a rough attack. It soon came. The bear reared up, walked leisurely forward, and caught hold of the spit with one of his paws. He jerked it from the goblin's hand, and sent it spinning to the other end of the kitchen.

A fierce battle ensued. This way and that flew tables and chairs, and pots and pans. The elf was one moment on the bear's back pulling his ears and pummeling his body with fists and heels; and a moment later the bear had thrown the skrattel up in the air, and when he came down treated him with a hug that made the little imp squall. Then the skrattel would jump up on one of the beams out of Bruin's reach; and soon, watching his chance, would leap down astride of the bear's neck.

Meantime Anders had become sadly frightened. Presently he observed that the oven door was open, and he crept in for shelter from the fray and lay there anxious and trembling. The struggle went on for a long time, and it was not at all clear who would be the winner. The whole house rang with the noise of the biting, scratching, snarling, screeching, growling, and pounding. At last, however, the elf seemed to be growing weaker. The rivals had paused for a moment to get breath, and the bear was about to attack again when the skrattel dashed his red cap right in the bear's eyes, and while Bruin was half blinded and smarting with the blow, the imp darted to the door and was gone from sight into the night, though the wind blew in a gusty gale, and the rain was falling in torrents.

"Well done! Bravo, Bruin!" the huntsman cried, as he crawled out of the oven and ran and bolted the door. "You have combed that fellow's locks finely, though you yourself are also rather the worse for the battle. But come; let us make the best of the good cheer our friend has left us."

Accordingly, they set the overturned table on its legs, put the room somewhat to rights, brought the roasted kid from the nook of the fireplace where it had escaped harm, and enjoyed a hearty feast. When they finished, the huntsman jovially wished the skrattel a good night and pleasant dreams, and lay down and slept till sunrise. Bruin slept also, as well as his aching bones would let him.

In the morning the huntsman made ready to continue on his journey. Scarcely had he set foot on the highway when he met the woodman, who eagerly inquired how he had passed the night. Anders described the elf, and told how the bear had vanquished him. "I fancy," Anders said in conclusion, "that you are now well rid of the gentleman. He is not likely to come where he thinks he runs the risk of getting any more of Bruin's hugs. If we have driven away the skrattel you are amply rewarded for your entertainment of us, which, to tell the truth, was none of the best; for if your ugly little tenant had not brought his supper with him we should have empty stomachs this morning."

So saying, the huntsman and Bruin, his fellow traveler, journeyed on. Let us hope they reached the king of Denmark safely, but as to their further adventures I know nothing.

The woodman, in the days that followed, kept sharp watch of his old house to determine whether the skrattel would return, or whether the bear had thoroughly frightened him out of his former haunt. Three nights passed, and the house showed no traces of the skrattel's having revisited it, and the woodman began to think of moving back. On the fourth day, while at work in the forest, a chilly scud of sleet and rain drove him to the shelter of a tree. As he stood there leaning against the tree-trunk he heard a little cracked voice singing, or rather croaking, for the singer's tone and the words of the song were equally mournful. The woodman crept quietly along in the direction whence the sound came, and presently peeped over some bushes and saw, seated on a mossy tussock, the very same little man whom the huntsman had described to him. The goblin had no hat or cap on his head, his face was woe-begone, and his legs were scratched as if he had been crawling through a bramble thicket. He was evidently sadly in the dumps at the loss of the good cheer and shelter of the woodman's cottage.

"Sing us another verse," the woodman said, when the song came to an end.

Instantly the little imp jumped up, stamped his feet with rage, and was out of sight in the twinkling of an eye.

The woodman finished his work and was going home in the evening, trudging along by his horse's side, when he saw the little goblin standing on a high bank beside the road, looking as grim and sulky as before.

"Hark ye, bumpkin," the skrattel cried, "is your great cat alive and at home still?"

"My cat?" the woodman said wonderingly.

"Yes, your great cat!" the little imp shouted wrathfully.

Then it occurred to the woodman that the skrattel was referring to the bear. "Oh, to be sure, my cat," the woodman said. "Certainly, she is alive and well, and would be happy to see you whenever you will do us the favor to call. And as you seem to be so fond of my great cat, you may like to know that she had five kittens last night."

"Five kittens!" the elf muttered.

"Yes," the woodman said, "five of the most beautiful kits you ever saw, and so like the old cat! It would do your heart good to see the whole family. They have such soft, gentle paws, such delicate whiskers, and such pretty little mouths! Do look in tonight about twelve o'clock—the time, you know, that you used to come to see us. I can assure you that the old cat will be glad to show you her kittens."

"I come? Not I, indeed!" the skrattel shrieked. "What do I want with the little wretches? Did not I see the mother once? Keep your kittens to yourself. I must be off. This is no place for me. Five kittens! So there are six of the vicious brutes now! Goodbye to you. You've seen me for the last time. So bad luck to your ugly cats and beggarly house! "

"And bad luck to you, Mr. Crookback!" the woodman cried. "Keep clear of my cat, and let us hear no more of your pranks, and be hanged to you!"

Now that he knew his troublesome guest had gone for good, the woodman moved back into the snug old house with his wife and children, his dog, and his white cat with her five kittens. There they lived happily, for the skrattel never came to see them any more.

THE FIGHT BETWEEN THE BEAR AND THE SKRATTEL

SNOW-WHITE, ROSE-RED
AND THE BIG BLACK BEAR

A POOR WIDOW once lived in a little cottage with a garden in front of it. and in the garden grew two rose bushes, one bearing white roses and the other red. The widow had two little girls who were just like the flowers that bloomed on the rose bushes, and she called one Snow-white, and the other Rose-red. They were the sweetest and best children in the world, always industrious and always cheerful. But Snow-white was quieter and gentler than Rose-red, for Rose-red loved to run about the fields and meadows, picking flowers and chasing butterflies, while Snow- white was more inclined to stay in the house and help her mother.

The two children loved each other so dearly that they always walked hand in hand when they went out together, and often one would say, "We will never desert each other," and the other would respond, "No, not as long as we live."

If the mother was within hearing she would add,

"Whatever one gets she will share with the other."

They delighted to roam about in the woods gathering berries, and no beast ever harmed them. Neither did any beast fear them. The rabbits would eat cabbage leaves from their hands, the deer grazed beside them in the most confiding manner, and the birds remained perched on the boughs close by, singing as if nobody was near. No evil befell them, even if they tarried so late in the forest that darkness overtook them and they could not get home that night. In that case, they would lie down on the moss and sleep till morning, and their mother knew they were quite safe, and never felt anxious about them.

Once, when they had passed the night in the forest, and had been wakened by the rising sun, they saw a beautiful child dressed in shining garments sitting near their resting place. The child got up, looked at them kindly, and without saying anything vanished among the trees. When they looked round them they became aware that they had slept close to the edge of a precipice. They ran home and told their mother of this adventure, and she said that the child in shining raiment must have been an angel guarding them from danger.

Snow-white and Rose-red kept their mother's cottage so clean and tidy that it was a pleasure to go into it. Every morning in the summer-time Rose-red, after putting the house in order, would gather a nosegay for her mother, and in this she always placed a bud from each rosebush.

Every winter's morning Snow-white would light the fire and put the kettle on to boil, and though the kettle was made of brass it was so well scoured that it shone like gold. In the evenings, when the frosty winds were scurrying over the bare fields and through the leafless trees, the little family would sit by the warm fireside, and the mother would put on her spectacles and read aloud out of an interesting book while her children were spinning. Beside them on the floor lay a little lamb, and behind them perched a small white dove with its head tucked under its wing.

One evening as they sat thus cozily together there came a knock at the door, and the mother said: "Make haste, Rose-red, and open the door. Very likely some poor wanderer is seeking shelter."

So Rose-red unbarred and opened the door expecting to find a man outside, but, instead, a great black bear poked in his head. Rose- red gave a startled scream and sprang back, the lamb began to bleat, the dove fluttered on its perch, and Snow-white ran and hid behind her mother's bed. "Don't be afraid," the bear said. "I won't hurt you. I am half frozen and only wish to warm myself."

"You poor bear," the mother said. "I think you had

better lie down by the fire; but take care not to burn your fur."

Then she spoke to her children. "Come back to your spinning," she said. "The bear is a good honest fellow who will do you no harm."

So they returned to the hearth, and the bear said, "Children, I wish you would brush the snow from my fur."

Then they fetched their brooms and brushed him off. After that the beast stretched himself in front of the fire and was quite happy and comfortable. In a little while the children became familiar enough to play tricks on their shaggy guest. They pulled his fur, climbed over him, and even ventured to beat him with a hazel-stick. If he growled they only laughed. The bear submitted to everything good-naturedly, but when they went too far he cried out:—

"Spare my life, you children,

Snow-white and Rose-red,

Don't beat your good friend dead."

When it was time to retire for the night, and the children had gone to bed, the mother said to the bear, "You can sleep on the hearth, if you like, and so be safely protected from the rough winter weather."

As soon as day dawned the children let the bear out, and he trotted away over the snow into the wood, but he returned in the evening, and thus it was every day for a longtime. Always when he came into the house he lay down on the hearth, and he let the children play what pranks they pleased with him. Even the lamb and the dove gradually recovered from their fears. He became like one of the family, and the door was never bolted for the night until he arrived.

When spring came, and everything outdoors was green again, the bear one morning said to Snow-white, "Now I must go away, and I shall not return until the summer is past."

"Where are you going, dear bear?" Snow-white asked.

"I must go to the forest and guard my treasures from the wicked dwarfs," he said. "In winter, when the earth is frozen hard, they are obliged to remain underground; but now they are beginning to come up to spy the land and steal all they can. What they once get possession of they conceal in their caves, and it is not easily recovered." Snow-white was quite sad as she unbarred the door, and watched the bear hurry away and disappear among the trees.

A short time after this the mother sent the children into the wood to gather fagots. In their wanderings they came to a tree which lay on the ground. Near the roots, at some distance from where they were, they saw something on the tree-trunk that kept bobbing up and down, and they could not imagine what it was. They went closer and saw that the strange object was a dwarf with a wizened face, and a white beard a yard long. The end of the beard was caught in a cleft of the tree, and the little man jumped about like a dog at the end of a string. He evidently did not know how to free himself, and he glared at the girls with his fiery red eyes, and cried out: "What are you standing there for? Can't you come and help me? "

"What are you doing, little man?" Rose-red asked.

"You stupid, inquisitive goose!" the dwarf exclaimed. "I wanted to split the tree and cut it up into wood proper for my kitchen fire. The great sticks which you use would burn up our food in no time. We don't need to cook such a quantity as you greedy folk. But the wedge I drove into the tree-trunk flew out, and the crack closed and caught my beautiful beard. So here I am, unable to get away; and you silly milk-and-water girls just stand and laugh. Ugh! What wretches you are!"

The children tried to pull the dwarf's beard out, but they did not succeed. "I will run and fetch help," Rose-red said at length.

"Crack-brained sheep's head that you are!" the dwarf snarled. "What is the use of calling any one else? You girls are two too many for me now. Can you think of nothing better than that?"

"Don't be so impatient," Snow-white said. "I know what to do," and she took her scissors out of her pocket and snipped off his beard close down to where it was caught in the log.

As soon as the dwarf felt himself at liberty he snatched up a bag full of gold that lay among the tree roots and marched off grumbling and groaning. "Stupid wretches!" he said, "they have cut off a piece of my beautiful beard. Plague take them!" And away he hurried without as much as looking at the children again.

Not many days later, Snow-white and Rose-red went to a pond a-fishing. As they approached the fishing-place they saw something which looked like an enormous grasshopper jumping about on the shore. They ran forward and recognized their old acquaintance, the dwarf. "What are you trying to do?" Rose-red asked. "Surely you are not going to jump into the water."

"I'm not such a simpleton as to do that," the dwarf retorted. "Don't you see that a horrid fish is trying to drag me in?"

The little man had been sitting on the bank fishing, when, unfortunately, the wind had entangled his beard in the line. Then a big fish got on his hook, and the weak little fellow had not the strength to draw the fish out. The fish was having the best of the struggle, and though the dwarf grabbed at the reeds and bushes, he was being dragged nearer and nearer the water. The girls arrived just in time to prevent a catastrophe. They caught hold of him, and held him firm and tried to disentangle his beard from the line, but in vain. So Snow-white took out her scissors again and sacrificed another portion of his beard.

When the dwarf perceived what she had done, he was in a great rage and exclaimed: "You donkey! Do you call that manners to thus disfigure a fellow's face? Wasn't it enough that you shortened my beard before? I can't appear before my own people like this. I wish you'd been at Jericho first." Then he took up a bag of pearls that lay among the rushes, and without another word dragged it away and disappeared.

It happened soon after this that the mother sent the two maidens to the next town to buy thread, needles, and ribbons. Their road passed over a heath where huge boulders of rock lay scattered about. While trudging along they saw a broad-winged eagle hovering in the air above them. Presently it made a quick descent and alighted on a rock not far away. Immediately afterward they heard a piercing shriek. They ran forward and saw with horror that the eagle had pounced upon the dwarf whom they had met twice before, and was about to carry him off. The children thereupon laid hold of the little man, and held him fast till the bird gave up the struggle and flew away.

No sooner had the dwarf recovered from his fright than he exclaimed in his squeaking voice: "You toads! Couldn't you have held me more carefully? You have torn my coat all to shreds, useless, awkward hussies that you are!"

So saying, he shouldered a bag filled with precious stones and hastened into his cave under the rocks.

The girls went on their way and did their errands in the town. They had turned homeward and were again on the heath, just before sundown, when they came unawares on the dwarf pouring out his precious stones on an open space, for he had thought no one would pass at so late an hour. The low rays of the sun shone on the stones, which sparkled and glanced so beautifully that the children stopped to admire them.

"What are you standing there gaping for?" the dwarf screamed, and his face became scarlet with rage.

He was continuing his abusive words when a sudden growl was heard, and a great black bear came shambling forth from among the rocks. The dwarf started to run, but before he could reach his cave the bear overtook him. "Spare me, dear Mr. Bear," he cried in terror. "I will give you all my treasures. Look at those beautiful precious stones lying there. What pleasure would you get from eating a poor, feeble little fellow like me? You wouldn't feel me between your teeth. But here are two wicked girls—take them. They would make tender morsels for you. They are fat as young quails. Eat them, for heaven's sake."

The bear, however, paid no attention to the dwarf's words, and gave the evil little creature such a blow with his paw that he never stirred again.

The maidens had started to run away, but the bear called after them: "Snow-white and Rose-red, don't you know me? You need not be afraid. I am the black bear you befriended last winter. Wait and I will go home with you." *

They recognized his voice, and they stopped and waited till he came to where they were. Then, to their astonishment, his shaggy skin suddenly fell off, and a young prince stood before them, dressed in the richest clothes. "That dwarf had enchanted me and stolen all my wealth," the prince said, "and I was condemned to wander about in the form of a bear till the dwarf's death should set me free. Now he has received his well-merited punishment."

Then they went to the children's home, and though on the next day the prince departed to go to his father's palace, he frequently visited the cottage in the years that followed. When Snow-white grew up he married her, and his brother married Rose-red. The two brothers shared equally the immense treasure the dwarf had collected, and they dwelt together in the palace they had inherited from their father.

Snow-white and Rose-red enjoyed their beautiful home, and they had their mother come to live with them. She brought with her the two rose-bushes which had been in the cottage yard, and at her request these were planted in front of the palace, where, every year, they bore the finest white and red roses.

THE BEAR COMES TO THE AID OF THE MAIDENS

The Bears And The Magician

Once AN OLD INDIAN magician was walking through the forest when he saw a great company of wolves gathered in a circle about one of their number who was evidently their chief. The old magician drew near and said, "Wolf chief, I am often hungry and unable to secure food. Pity me and make me into a wolf that I may live as you do and catch deer and other animals that are swift of foot."

"Come hither, then," the wolf chief responded, "and I will rub you with my paws so that you will be hairy as we are."

"No, no," the old magician said, "I would not have my entire body covered with hair, but only my arms and legs."

So the chief wolf rubbed only the arms and legs of the old magician, and they were immediately covered with shaggy hair. Then the chief wolf ordered some of his followers to go with the stranger to help him hunt, and they went with him up among the high mountains where it was very cold. At night they lay down to sleep, and the old magician was chilled through and through by the frosty wind. "Cover me with your tails," he said to the wolves; and they lay down around him and covered him with their bushy tails. So he soon became warm and slept.

When it was daylight they resumed their hunting, and by and by they saw some moose. They gave chase and quickly overtook and killed them. Scarcely had they begun eating their prey when the chief wolf and a numerous troop of followers came along to share in the feast. The old magician gnawed the meat from a bone and threw the bone away, and by some mischance it hit and killed one of the wolves.

"You cannot stay with us or in this region any longer," the chief wolf said. "You must go where we will not see you again. But I will not be too severe, for one of my wolves shall be your companion and assist you to hunt." So the old magician and his single wolf attendant went off and lived by themselves, and they killed all the elk and deer and moose they wanted.

One day a deer that the wolf was chasing took refuge on an island in the middle of the stream. The wolf followed, but as soon as he entered the brush along the shore of the island a bear seized and killed him.

The magician waited a long time for the wolf to return, and then went to look for him. He asked all the birds and other creatures he saw if they could tell him what had become of his wolf, but none of then could give him any information until he accosted a kingfisher who was sitting on a limb overhanging a stream.

"Why do you sit there, my friend?" the old magician asked.

"I am looking for something to eat," the kingfisher replied. "A little way up this stream is an island that is the home of the chief bear and his two brothers. One of them has killed your wolf, and now they are eating him, but they only care for the lean meat, and they throw the fat into the water. Whenever I see a piece come floating along I fly down and get it."

"I suppose," the magician said, "that the bears have on the island some sort of a cave or den in which they spend most of their time. Do they often come out?"

"They come out every morning," the kingfisher responded, "and play on the sandy shore."

The old magician went to the island and saw the bears' tracks in the sand where it was their custom to play, and he turned himself into a dry dead tree on the adjacent bank. There he waited till the bears appeared.

When they saw the tree the chief bear said: "Look

at that dead tree. It is the old magician. Brothers, go and see if it is not." So the two brothers of the chief bear went to the tree and clawed it, but the old magician never moved or cried out. "No," they said, "it is only a tree."

Then the chief bear went and clawed and bit the tree, and although this hurt the old magician sadly he never moved or cried out. That made the chief bear sure that the tree was really a tree, and he began to play with his brothers. As they were rolling about, the old magician assumed his human form, leaned over the edge of the bank, and shot a well-aimed arrow into each of the three bears, and they fell lifeless on the sand.

Afterward he crossed to the mainland and walked down beside the stream. Pretty soon he met a frog leaping hastily along in the opposite direction. Every time the frog jumped it would say, "Chief Bear"; and occasionally it would stop and add, "I bring healing to Chief Bear and his brothers."

"Ha!" the old magician exclaimed, "tell me what you mean by that?"

"Why, they have been killed," the frog said, "and I am going to give them some medicine that will make them as much alive as ever."

"No, you are not," the magician declared, and he spoke so threateningly that the frog turned back.

Then the magician retraced his steps to the island. "I will not have those rascally bears restored to life," he said.

So he made a big fire, skinned the bears, and roasted the meat in such a way that all the grease ran into a hollow of the ground. That done, he summoned all the animals in the forest to come and roll in the pool of grease, and promised them that this oily bath would make them fat.

The bears came first and rolled in the grease, and that is the reason there is so much fat on a bear's body. Last of all came the rabbits. By that time the grease was nearly gone, but they filled their paws with it, and rubbed it on their backs and between their hind legs, and that is why every rabbit now is so fat in those places.

GRANDSIRE BEAR
AND REYNARD THE FOX

At DAWN one day Bruin came tramping over the bog with a fat pig on his shoulder, and scarcely had he finished crossing the bog when he was accosted by Reynard who was sitting on a wayside stone.

"Good day, grandsire," the fox said; "what's that so nice that you have there?"

"Pork," Bruin replied.

"Well, I have a dainty bit, too," Reynard said.

"What is it?" the bear asked, laying down his burden.

"The biggest wild bees' comb I ever saw in my life," Reynard declared.

"Indeed, you don't say so," Bruin said, and licked his .lips at thought of how good the honey would taste. "Will you swap it for my pork?" he asked, after meditating a few moments.

"No, no," Reynard responded. "I can't do that."

But after some further talk they agreed to each select and repeat the names of three trees. If the fox could say his three off faster than the bear could say his, he was to have leave to take one bite of the pig. But if the bear was the winner he was to have permission to take one sup out of the honeycomb; and Bruin was very sure he could get all the honey in that one sup.

Now they began to name the trees. "Fir, tamarack, larch," the bear growled. He was not angry, but his voice was always gruff, no matter how pleasant his mood.

"Ash, aspen, oak," Reynard cried; and he won, for Bruin had only named two trees.

"Larch and tamarack are different names for the same kind of tree," the fox said, and he pounced on the pig and took the heart out at one bite.

"You've taken the very best part of my pork," the bear snarled, and he made a grab at the fox, caught hold of his tail, and held him fast.

"Let me go," the fox begged. "I'll make amends. You shall have a taste of my honey."

When Bruin heard that, he loosed the fox, and away went Reynard after the honeycomb. He soon returned and held it up under the bear's nose, saying, "Here on this honeycomb lies a leaf, and under the leaf is a hole, and that hole you are to suck."

Bruin took the comb and put it up to his mouth, and the fox slipped off the leaf, leaped back a little distance, and began to laugh; for instead of a honeycomb he had handed the bear a hornet's nest as big as a man's head. It was full of hornets, and they swarmed out and settled on the bear and stung him about the eyes and ears and mouth and snout. He had such hard work to rid himself of them that he had no time to think of Reynard, who escaped without any punishment.

This experience with the hornets is the reason why Bruin has ever since been very much afraid of them.

THE FOX GAVE THE BEAR A HORNET'S NEST

THE YOUNG HUNTERS AND THE BEARS

In A SMALL HUT, right in the middle of the forest, lived a man and wife and their three sons and a daughter.

One winter morning, after a night of snow, the three sons started off to hunt. They kept together for some time, but presently came to a place where their path divided, and one trail led away to the right and another to the left. The youngest brother decided to follow the left-hand trail. The older brothers, however, went on by the right-hand trail, and they had not gone far when their dogs scented a bear and drove him out of the thicket where he was hiding. The bear ran across an open space, and the oldest brother shot an arrow that hit the bear in the head and killed him.

They took him up and carried him toward home, and at the fork of the path met the youngest brother, who was returning empty-handed.

When they reached the home hut they threw the bear down on the floor saying: "Father, here is a bear we killed. Now we can have a good dinner."

But the father only said, "When I was a young man, and my brothers and I went to hunt, we rarely got less than two bears in one day."

The sons were rather disappointed, because they had expected praise for their prowess, instead of criticism. There was plenty of meat to last for several days, but early the next morning they again started off hunting. They followed the same trail as before, and parted in like manner at the fork of the path. Soon a bear ran out from behind a tree in front of the two older brothers, and they and their dogs pursued and killed him. On their way back they met the youngest brother at the fork of the path, and he also had shot a bear on the left-hand trail.

They carried the two bears home, but when they threw them triumphantly on the floor of the hut their father only said, "My brothers and I often got three bears in one day."

So, in spite of the great supply of meat they now had, the sons again set forth to hunt the next morning, and they were lucky enough to each shoot a bear this time. But when they brought the three bears home their father said, "My brothers and I sometimes killed four bears in one day."

The bears the sons had shot were the servants of a great bear chief who lived in a cavern beneath a high mountain a long way off. This chief was furious because so many of his bears were being killed, and he determined to find some way of destroying the youthful hunters. So he said to one of his servants: "Go to the path that these youths frequent, and secrete yourself where it forks. When they and their dogs approach show yourself and induce them to chase you until you return here. The mountain will open to let you and your pursuers in, and then I shall have them in my power, and we shall be able to revenge ourselves."

The servant bowed low and hurried to the fork of the path, where he hid in the bushes. Only the two older brothers came forth to hunt that day. Suddenly their dogs began to bark loudly, and the bear sprang out of the thicket and scurried away in the direction of the mountain. The youths gave chase and followed him even till the mountain opened in front of them. They all rushed in pell-mell; nor did the lads slacken their headlong pace until they saw bears sitting on every side of them holding a council.

"Why are you trying to kill all my servants?" the bear chief asked, frowning at the two youths. "It is I who ordered the bear you have been chasing to lure you into my power to-day. I shall take care that you do not hurt my people any more, for you will become bears yourselves."

The youths cast frightened glances at the angry assemblage around them and saw only one bear who showed any compassion. That one was the bear chief's sister. She was sorry for the lads and begged the chief to be lenient.

"Very well," he said, "I will not be as severe as I at first intended. Their heads and bodies shall remain as they are, and only their arms and legs shall be changed into those of a bear; but they will have to go on all fours the rest of their lives."

As he spoke he stooped over a spring of water that bubbled up in the mountain cavern, drew forth a handful of moss, and rubbed it over the arms and legs of the lads. Instantly the transformation took place, and they were neither beast nor human.

The bear chief knew that their father would seek for his sons when they did not return home, and he sent one of his servants to hide at the fork of the path and see what the man did.

This servant was very cunning, and he took along the snowshoes of one of the lads. There had been a light fall of snow since they came to the mountain, and it had covered up their tracks. When the bear got to where the path divided he put the snowshoes on his hind feet, stood upright, and walked along the right-hand trail to the edge of a precipice. There he arranged some brush so that the precipice would not be easily perceived, and then he ran back to the fork of the path and hid.

Soon the father came in sight, stooping as he walked to look for his sons' tracks in the snow. When he saw the marks of snowshoes on the right-hand path he was filled with joy, and hastened eagerly forward. He had no thought of danger, and he plunged headlong down the precipice and was killed.

Again the bear arranged some concealing brush at the edge of the declivity, and returned to his hiding-place.

The mother at home was meanwhile becoming more and more anxious over the long absence of her two sons, and when her husband did not come back promptly she said she would go forth and try to find him and them.

"No, let me undertake the search," her youngest son begged.

"You must stay at home and take care of your sister," she said, and she put on her snowshoes and started.

She followed her husband's tracks, and like him plunged down the precipice and was killed.

Then the bear went back to the mountain and reported to his chief.

Hour after hour dragged heavily by in the forest hut, and at last the brother and sister felt quite sure that in some way or other the rest of the family had perished. Every morning the youth climbed to the top of a tall tree near the house, and sat there till he was almost frozen, looking about in all directions, hoping that he might see some of the lost ones returning. At last the food in the hut had all been eaten, and he could no longer delay going to hunt for more.

His sister did not like to be left alone in the hut and cried bitterly when he explained to her the necessity of seeking food.

"But surely," he said, "there is no use of sitting down quietly to starve; and whether find game or not I shall come back, so as not to be away overnight."

He spent an entire day getting ready. First he cut himself some arrows, each from a different tree, and winged every arrow with the feathers of four different birds, and afterward he made a very light, strong bow, and got his snowshoes ready.

Early the next morning he called his dog and set out. For a long time he went on and on, and at last he sat down on the fallen branch of a big oak tree to rest.

His dog ran round and round the tree barking furiously. The youth could see no reason for the dog's excitement, and began to fancy that the tree had let fall the branch and killed his brothers or parents. So with a vengeful feeling in his heart he shot one of his arrows at the tree. Thereupon he was startled by a noise like thunder, the tree shook from top to bottom, and burst into flames. In a few minutes nothing remained where it had stood but a heap of ashes.

The youth knew not what to make of the occurrence and after puzzling over it for a while he went on. Soon he came to a patch of bushes, and his dog dashed along the edge of it, barking loudly. A bear rushed out and sped away toward the mountains as fast as it could go, with the dog following close behind.

The lad gave chase also, but presently the thong of one of his snowshoes broke, and he had to stop to mend it. That allowed the dog and bear to get so far ahead he could hardly hear the dog's barking.

"Now," he said to his snowshoes, "you must go as fast as you can, or I shall lose the dog as well as the bear."

He hurried forward with all possible speed, and by and by came to the mountain that was the home of the bear chief, and which the bear and dog had already entered. The bear chief's sister was looking out of a window, and she could not help pitying the young lad just as she had his brothers. He wondered much over the disappearance of the two animals, but while he paused to think what he would do next he fancied he heard the dog's voice on the opposite side of the mountain.

With great difficulty he scrambled up the steep

rocks and forced his way through tangled thickets. When he reached the other side the dog's barking seemed to proceed from the place whence he had come. So he started back; but at the very top of the mountain, where he stopped to rest, he observed that the barking was directly beneath him. Instantly he knew where he was and what had happened.

"Let my dog out at once, bear chief!" he cried. "If you do not, I shall destroy your palace."

But the bear chief only laughed and said nothing.

This made the boy very angry, and when he had descended the mountain he turned and shot an arrow straight at it. Immediately there was a deep rumbling sound, flames broke out, and the whole mountain crumbled and was consumed. All the bears perished in the fire except the bear chief's sister. She was spared because she had tried to save the two elder lads from punishment.

As soon as the fire had burned itself out the young hunter went seeking for his brothers among the ruins of the mountain, and he soon found them, half bear, half human, coming toward him on all fours.

When they got to where he was they rose on their hind legs and put their shaggy forepaws on his shoulders, and the three cried together over the elder two's sad plight, which none of them knew how to remedy.

But now the bear chief's sister came gently to them and said to the young hunter: "Yonder is a spring. Take some moss from it, and you need only have your brothers smell the moss to restore them to their proper form."

All three ran to the spring, the youngest plucked a handful of wet moss, and the two others sniffed at it with all their might. Then their limbs became human, and they stood upright.

"What can we do for you to show our gratitude?" they said to the bear chief's sister.

She only smiled and sent them home to look after their sister who was in the forest hut alone with no one to protect her.

THE BEAR

AND THE WRENS

One SUMMER'S DAY a bear and a wolf were taking a walk in a wood when they heard a bird singing very sweetly. "Brother Wolf," the bear said, "what kind of a bird is that which is singing so prettily?"

"That is the King of the Birds, before whom we must do reverence," the wolf replied; but really it was only a wren.

"If that is the King of the Birds," the bear said, "I would like to see his royal palace. Come, show it to me."

"I will show it to you as soon as the queen returns home," the wolf responded.

So they waited, and kept a sharp watch, and soon saw the queen go to her nest, which was in a crevice of a bank. She carried food in her beak for her young ones. A few moments later she flew away, and the wolf and bear went and peeped into the nest. They saw five or six young birds in it.

"Is that the royal palace?" the bear asked. "It is a wretched hole; and do you mean to say that those are royal children? They are miserable brats."

When the young wrens heard this they were furious, and they shrieked: "No, no! We are not. You shall be punished for your insulting words."

The bear and the wolf began to be afraid, and they went and hid themselves in their dens, but the young birds kept on screaming and making a terrible noise. As soon as their parents again brought them food the fledglings said, "We will not touch so much as the leg of a fly—no, not if we starve—till you have proved that we are respectable children. The bear has been calling us names. "

"There, there, my dears," their father said, "be quiet, and he shall be punished." So the father and mother birds flew to the bear's den and cried: "Old Growler, why have you insulted our children? You shall suffer for what you have done. We declare a fierce war on you."

The wrens flew away, and the bear made haste to summon his friends to his aid. All the four-footed beasts assembled—cattle, donkeys, elephants, lions, and every animal that walks the earth with four feet. Meanwhile, the wrens summoned all the creatures with wings—not only the birds, great and small, but gnats, hornets, bees, and flies.

The time came for the war to begin, and the father wren sent out spies to discover who was to be the general of the enemy's army. Among the spies were some gnats, and they were the most cunning of all. One of these gnats flew to a wood and discovered the four-footed beasts holding a council beneath a great tree. He alighted on a leaf of the tree and heard the bear say to the fox, "Reynard, you are famous for your slyness, so you shall be our general and lead us."

"Very good," the fox responded, "and now we must agree on a signal. I have a fine long bushy tail which looks very like a red feather at a distance. If I hold it straight up all is going well, and you are to march after me and charge the enemy. But if I allow it to hang down you must run for your lives."

When the fox finished speaking, the gnat flew back and told the father wren what had been said.

The battle morning dawned, and the four-footed beasts came rushing along roaring and bellowing, and making the very earth shake with their tread. The wren and his army came also, whirring through the air, screaming and flapping and buzzing enough to make you tremble in your shoes. Thus the two hosts advanced against each other, and the wren sent a hornet, to settle on the fox's tail and sting it as hard as possible.

The hornet did as it was ordered, and when the fox felt the sting he lifted a hind leg, but he bore the pain bravely and kept his tail in the air. Again the hornet stung, and the fox was forced to let his tail droop a little bit, but only a little. Then the hornet stung the third time, and down went the tail of the fox between his legs. The other beasts at once concluded that all was lost, and they began to run each to its own hole.

So the birds won the battle, and the wren and his wife flew home to their children and said: "Now be happy. Eat and drink to your hearts' content, for we are the victors."

But the young wrens said, "We will not touch a thing until the bear has been to the nest and begged our pardon and admitted that we are respectable children."

The parent wrens therefore flew to the bear's den, and cried, "Old Growler, you must come to our nest and beg pardon of our little ones for calling them names, or you shall be punished."

Their threat terrified the bear greatly, and he came crawling to the nest and apologized. Then, at last, the young wrens were satisfied, and they ate, drank, and made merry till far into the night.

THE BEAR AND THE TWO HUNTSMEN

TWO HUNTSMEN who were in need of money went to a fur dealer to sell him a bearskin. But they could not show him the skin, for as yet it was on a live bear that rambled free in the forest. However, they promised that they would soon kill the creature and bring his hide to the fur dealer's shop.

"And he is a very king of bears," they declared, "the biggest bear under the sun. We would wager that his skin is cheap at double the price we ask. It will make two robes where an ordinary skin would only make one."

Never did any one prize a pelt as they did their bearskin, for they seemed to think they owned it rather than the bear, and they succeeded in persuading the dealer to buy it.

"We will bring it to you in two days at most," they promised.

Forth they went with their guns, but it was easier to find the bear than to get his skin; for he suddenly came out of a thicket growling threateningly, and approached them at a trot. Such an unexpected course on the part of the bear greatly alarmed our two hunters, and one of them, who was very light and nimble, hastily clambered up a tree. The other, cold as ice with fear, fell on his face, held his breath, and pretended he was dead, for he had heard that a bear would not molest a dead person.

Such a blockhead was the bear that he actually believed that the man lying there full length on the ground was a corpse; yet he half-suspected some deceit, and he smelt and snuffed the prostrate hunter from head to foot. "Yes, yes, the fellow's dead," the bear muttered, "and his decaying flesh has an odor that is far from sweet. Well, I'll leave the body where it is, to be devoured by the carrion crows."

Then off he shambled into the woods. After the bear had disappeared, the hunter in the tree cautiously descended, and went to his companion lying in the dirt. He helped him up and said consolingly: "It is not surprising that the monster forced us asunder, and we can rejoice that we are more scared than hurt. But how about the creature's skin?" he asked with a smile and a jovial wink. "I observed that the bear held his muzzle very close to your ear—what did he whisper to you?"

The other replied thus, "He gave this caution—Never dare Again to sell the skin of bear Its owner has not ceased to wear.'"

Bruin Outwitted

Once UPON A TIME there was a bear who lay down on a hillside in the sun and slept. By and by Reynard came slouching along and caught sight of him. "There lies Grandsire Bruin taking his ease," the fox said. "I think I'll play him a trick."

So he caught a field mouse, put it on a stump close to Bruin's head, and bawled into the bear's ear, "Wake up, Bruin, and look out for the hunters!"

Then he ran off into the woods as fast as he could go.

Bruin awoke with a start, and when he saw the little mouse on the stump he lifted his paw to strike and crush it, for he thought the mouse was the one who had been bellowing into his ear.

Just at that moment he caught sight of Reynard running away through the bushes, and knew it was the fox instead of the mouse who had disturbed his slumbers so rudely. Off he went after him with such a rush that the under wood crackled as he went. He gained on Reynard, and presently was so close to him that he caught hold of his hind foot as he was crawling into a hole under a pine root.

Reynard was fairly in the grip of his enemy, but he nevertheless kept his wits about him, and yelled, "Let go of the pine root and catch Reynard's foot!"

So the bear, in his excitement, released the foot of the fox, and laid hold of the root, while Reynard slipped down into the hole beyond reach.

"I got the best of you that time, Grandsire," the fox called back.

"Out of sight isn't out of mind," the bear growled down the hole, and then he went away enraged and disappointed.

The Bear's
Bad Bargain

Once UPON A TIME an old woodman lived with his wife in a tiny hut close to a rich man's orchard—so close, indeed, that some of the boughs of a pear tree in the orchard hung right over the cottage yard.

The rich man told the woodman and his wife that if any of the fruit fell into their yard they might have it to eat, and they watched the pears ripening with hungry eyes. As the time drew near when the rich man would have the pears picked they could not help wishing that a storm of wind or some other chance would cause the fruit to fall. But the pears continued to hang on the drooping branches, and there seemed to be little prospect that the cottage dwellers would get more than a meager few.

This was quite irritating to the old wife, and she grumbled and scolded, and took to giving her husband nothing but dry bread to eat. At the same time she insisted on his working harder than ever, so that the poor old woodman got quite thin.

At last he declared that he would work no more unless his wife gave him some good rich soup for his dinner.

So the old woman took some rice and pulse and some butter and spices, and began to cook a savory soup. What an appetizing smell it had, to be sure! If the woodman could have had his way he would have stayed in the house to be ready to gobble up the soup as soon as it was ready.

But the old wife said: "No, no, you shall have none of the soup till you have brought home another load of wood. And it must be a good-sized load, too. You have got to work for your dinner."

It was of no use to argue, and the old man went off to the forest where he hacked and hewed with such a will that he soon had quite a large bundle of sticks.

Just then a bear came swinging along, peering about with his keen little eyes. "Peace be with you, friend," the bear said. "What are you going to do with that remarkably large bundle of wood?"

"It is for my wife," the woodman answered. "The fact is, she has made a splendid soup for dinner, and if I bring home a good bundle of wood she is pretty sure to give me a plentiful portion of soup. Oh, my dear fellow, you should just smell that soup! "

At this the bear's mouth began to water, and he said, "Do you think your wife would give me some of it, if I brought her a bundle of wood?"

"Perhaps she would if you brought her a very big load," the woodman responded.

"Would four hundred weight be enough?" the bear asked anxiously.

"I'm afraid not," the woodman said, shaking his head. "You see such a soup as she is making is expensive. There is rice in it, and lots of butter, and pulse, and—"

"Would eight hundred weight do?" the bear interrupted.

"Say half a ton, and it's a bargain," the woodman answered.

"Half a ton is a large quantity," the bear sighed.

"There are spices in the soup," the woodman said.

The bear licked his lips, and his little eyes twinkled greedily. "Well," he said, "I'll get the wood, and you go home and tell your wife to keep the soup hot till I come."

Away went the woodman in great glee, and informed his wife of how the bear had agreed to bring half a ton of wood in return for a share of the soup.

The wife acknowledged that her husband had made a good bargain. "But you ought to have settled exactly what share of the soup the bear was to have," she said; "for if the three of us sit down to eat together he will gobble up all there is in the pot before we have finished our first helping."

The woodman turned pale with alarm. "In that case," he said, "we had better begin now and have a fair start."

So, without more ado, they commenced to eat the soup as fast as they could.

"Wife," the woodman said, speaking with his mouth full, "remember to leave some for the bear."

"Certainly, certainly," she said, scooping up another dish of the savory soup.

Thus they went on eating and cautioning each other until not a morsel was left in the pot.

"What is to be done now?" the woodman said. "It is all your fault, wife, for eating so greedily."

"My fault!" his wife retorted scornfully, "why you ate twice as much as I did."

"No, I didn't!" he said.

"Yes, you did!" she repeated. "Men always eat more than women."

"Well," the woodman said, "it is of no use to quarrel about it now. The soup is gone, and the bear will be furious."

"We must lock up everything in the house that is good to eat," the old woman said, "and then hide in the garret."

So they made haste to lock up all the food, and went to the garret and hid.

Meanwhile the bear had been toiling and moiling away getting his half ton of wood. It took him much longer than he expected. However, the wood was at last ready, and he carried it to the woodcutter's cottage, where he arrived quite exhausted. He threw the load down and went in and saw the brass soup pot by the fire. Mercy! how angry he was when he found nothing in it—not even a grain of rice, nor a tiny bit of pulse, but only a smell so uncommonly nice that he cried with rage and disappointment. He flew around and turned the furniture topsy-turvy, yet he could not find a morsel of food.

"If I'm to go hungry," he said, "they shall have none of the wood I brought. I will carry it away."

But when he went out and looked at the bundle, and recalled how heavy it was, he did not care to burden himself with it again, even for the sake of revenge.

"At any rate, I won't go off empty-handed," he said, and he stepped back into the house and seized the soup pot. "If I can't get the taste I'll have the smell," he declared.

When he came out this time he caught sight of the beautiful yellow pears hanging over into the yard, and in a trice he clambered onto the wall and up the tree.

He picked one of the biggest and ripest pears, and was about to put it in his mouth when a thought struck him. "If I take these pears home," he said, "I shall be able to sell them for ever so much to the other bears, and with the money I can buy some soup. Ha, ha! I shall have the best of the bargain after all!" Then he began to gather the ripe pears as fast as he could and put them into the soup pot. Occasionally he came to an unripe one. "None of the bears would buy that," he would say with a shake of his head, "yet it is a pity to waste it."

So he would pop it into his mouth and eat it, making wry faces over its sourness.

All this time the woodman's wife had been watching the bear through a crevice, scarcely daring to breathe for fear of discovery. But she was asthmatic and had a cold in her head, and presently, just as the soup pot was full of ripe yellow pears, she gave the most tremendous sneeze you ever heard—*Ali-chew*!

The bear thought some one had fired a gun at him, and he dropped the soup pot into the cottage yard, and fled to the forest as fast as his legs would carry him.

Thus the woodman and his wife got the soup, the half ton of wood, and the coveted pears, but the poor bear got nothing except a very bad stomach-ache from eating unripe fruit.

THE WOODSMAN SPOKE WITH THE BEAR

THE BEAR IN A FOREST PITFALL

ONCE UPON A TIME there was a man who lived far, far away in the forest where he had many goats and sheep. But his flock suffered greatly from Greylegs, the wolf, and at last the man said, "I must trap this thieving Greylegs."

So one winter day he went to work digging a large square pitfall, and when he made the hole deep enough he set up a pole in the middle, and on the top of the pole fastened a board, and on the board he put a little dog. Over the pit itself he spread boughs and twigs and leaves, and on this covering strewed snow, so that Greylegs might not suspect there was a pit underneath.

When the man finished these arrangements he went home. By and by night came, and the little dog grew weary of sitting there, and began to bark at the moon. "Bow-wow, bow-wow!" he said.

Soon a fox came slouching and sneaking along.

He saw the little dog and thought that here was a fine chance for getting something to eat. So he gave a jump and went head over heels down into the pit. That frightened into silence the dog on the board at the top of the pole.

Later in the night the little dog got so weary and so hungry that he resumed his yelping and howling. "Bow-wow, bowwow!" he cried.

His barking presently attracted Greylegs, who came trotting to the spot, and was rejoiced to find a good meal ready for him. He leaped forward to seize the dog, and went head over heels into the pit.

The dog was again terrified into silence, but toward dawn the wind began to blow, and the air grew so cold that the little dog shivered and shook, and he barked with all his might for help—"Bow-wow, bowwow, bow-wow!"

His yelping was heard by a bear who was tramping along not far away, thinking how he could get a morsel for breakfast. "Well," he said, as he came to where he could see the dog, "here is my breakfast waiting for me." He hurried forward to seize the dog, and down he went with a crash and a bump through the concealing boughs and twigs head over heels into the pit.

The dog stopped howling, but for only a little while, he was so very chilly and weary and hungry. At length the sun rose and sent its rays glinting down into the snowy forest. Then came an old woman walking along through the wood. She was a beggar who toddled from farm to farm with a bag on her back.

As soon as she heard the dog she was curious to learn what he was doing there in the woodland, and why he barked in such distress. When she drew near she saw that he had been put there to lure some of the wild forest creatures into a pit, and she wondered if any beasts had been trapped during the night. A few paces from the edge of the pit she got down on her hands and knees and crept cautiously forward and peeped down into it.

"Here you are trapped at last, Reynard," she said to the fox, who was the first of the captives that she saw. "This is a very good place for such a hen roost robber as you are."

Then she observed the wolf and said: "Yes, and for you also, Greylegs. Many a goat and sheep have you caught and killed. Now you will receive your just punishment. Bless my heart! Are you here, too, Bruin, you horse-slayer. This very day you shall die, and that shaggy skin of yours will be nailed up on the wall to dry."

All this the old woman screeched out as she bent low at the edge of the pit, looking down into the gloom. But just as she finished her remarks the bag on her back slipped forward over her head with a jerk that carried her with it down into the pit.

So now there were four in the pit, and they each sat in a corner and glared at one another. Presently Reynard began to twist and turn and peer about, trying to discover some way to get out.

"Sit still, you whirligig thief!" the old woman cried. "Do as Bruin does. There he sits as grave as a judge."

She thought the bear's friendship was worth cultivating under the circumstances, and she hoped her compliment would win his favor.

But now the man arrived who owned the pitfall. First he drew up the old woman, and afterward he slew the three beasts. So he was troubled no more by Reynard or Greylegs or Bruin, and his flocks throve much better then ever before.

A BEAR STORY

IN NURSERY LATIN

As I was going up stin-dum-stair-um I met a high-gig-gle-y-bon-bear-um carrying off my fin-dum-fair-um; and I said, "I wish I had my gish-me-gair-um—I'd show that high-gig-gle-y--bon-bear-um how to carry off my fin-dum-fair-um!"

TRANSLATED INTO PLAIN ENGLISH

As I was going upstairs I met a bear carrying off my pig; and I said, "I wish I had my gun—I'd show that bear how to carry off my pig!"

The Bear Who Was
An Enchanted King

Once UPON A TIME there was a king who had three daughters. The less said about the elder two the better, but the third was the best tempered and most beautiful maiden in the kingdom, and the king and all his subjects were very fond of her.

One night she dreamed of a golden wreath which was so lovely that she declared, when she awoke, that she could not be happy until she had one just like it. She described it to her father, and he ordered the most skillful goldsmith who could be found, to make such a wreath. But when the wreath was ready it did not satisfy her, and she tossed it aside and grew so melancholy she would hardly say a word.

As she was walking one day in the woodland she saw a white bear who was playing with the very wreath of which she had dreamed.

"Will you sell me that wreath? " she asked.

"No," he said, "it is not for sale. But you can have it, if you will let me have you."

"Well," she responded, "then you can have me, for life without that golden wreath is not worth living."

He handed her the wreath, and said, "I will come to the palace to get you in three days' time."

When she returned home with the wreath every one was pleased to see her happy again. She told the king of her bargain with the white bear, and he declared that the bear should never have her. On the third day he ordered his army to guard the approaches to the palace, and to drive the bear away if he appeared.

By and by the bear came, but no one could withstand him. The soldiers' weapons had no effect on him, and he hurled the men who opposed him right and left so that they lay in heaps on either side.

The king saw that he must do something to appease the creature. He therefore sent out his eldest daughter to the bear, who took her on his back and went off. But they had not gone far when the bear asked, "Have you ever sat softer, and have you ever seen clearer?"

The princess replied, "I have sat softer on my mother's lap, and I have seen clearer in my father's hall."

"Oh!" the bear said, "then you are not the right

maiden"; and he ordered her to get off his back and go home.

Three days later the bear again went to the palace, and again the army attempted to drive him away, but he dashed the soldiers down like grass, and the king sent out to him his second daughter.

The white bear took her on his back and went off. Presently he asked, "Have you ever seen clearer, and have you ever sat softer?"

"In my father's hall I have seen clearer," she replied, "and on my mother's lap I have sat softer."'

"Oh, then you are not the right one!" the bear said. "Get off my back and go home."

Three days passed, and he once more went to the palace. The army tried to keep him back, but he tossed the soldiers hither and thither until the king saw how helpless the contest was, and sent out his youngest daughter.

The bear took her on his back and went away. When they had gone deep into the woodland he asked, "Have you ever sat softer or seen clearer?"

"No, never," she replied.

"Ah!" he said, "you are the right one."

After a while they came to a castle that was much grander than her father's palace.

"This is to be your home," the bear said, "and I hope you will live here happily. There will be nothing for you to do except to see that the fire never goes out."

The sun sank below the western horizon while he spoke, and to her surprise he became a man, and said his name was Valmon and that he was a king.

But when the sun came up in the east the next morning he was once more a bear and went away for the day.

Three years passed, and in all that time the white bear each evening became a man. He treated the princess kindly, and she loved him; but he was away every day, and she grew lonesome and at last begged leave to go home and see her parents.

"You may go," the bear said, "but do not remain more than three days."

So she went to her father's palace, and at the end of the three days prepared to return to the white bear. Her mother, however, urged her to stay one more night, and finally she consented.

The next day she went back to the splendid forest castle where she arrived in the evening just after the white bear had come home as usual to spend the night.

"Why did you stay away more than the three days?" he asked. "Now you have made us both unlucky. In another month should have been free from the enchantment that compels me to be a bear half the time. But your failure to do as I requested takes from me the power to transform myself into a man each evening. I have been bewitched by a hag of the trolls, and now I must go to her. She will restore my human shape and marry me."

He at once made ready to depart while the princess sat down and wept and moaned. Presently he finished his preparations and passed out of the door. Then the princess leaped to her feet and ran after him, caught hold of his shaggy hide, and threw herself on his back. There she held fast, and the bear carried her over hills and crags, and through brakes and briers till her clothes were torn to tatters, and she was so exhausted she fainted and let go her hold.

When she came to herself she was in a great wood, and she got up and wandered on, hoping to find the white bear. After a while she came to a hut, and in the doorway stood an old woman.

"Have you seen anything of King Valmon, the white bear?" the princess asked.

"Yes," the old woman said, "he passed by here this morning early, but he went so fast you'll never be able to catch up with him."

A little girl was running about in front of the hut playing with some golden scissors. She waved them about, clipping in the air, and, as she did so, splendid pieces of silk and satin cloth fell to the ground around her.

Plainly, whoever possessed those magic scissors could never lack fine raiment.

The princess was about to resume her journey when the little girl said to the old woman, "I would like to give my scissors to this stranger. She needs them more than I do."

The old woman was willing, and the princess went on her way with the magic scissors in her pocket. She walked and walked, and the next day came to another hut. An old woman stood in the doorway.

"Good-day," the princess said. "Have you seen anything of King Valmon the white bear?"

"Yes," the old woman replied, "he passed by yesterday, but he went so fast you will never be able to catch him."

On the floor, inside of the hut, a little girl was playing with a magic flask from which could be poured out any drink a person might wish to have. She rose and brought the flask to the princess. "Take it with you," she said. "You have a hard journey before you and need it more than I do."

So the princess accepted the flask and went on, and the next day came to a third hut. She greeted an old woman who stood in the doorway, and said, "Have you seen anything of King Valmon, the white bear?"

"He passed here day before yesterday," the old

woman replied, "and he went so fast you will never be able to overtake him."

On a bench beside the door a little girl was playing with a magic napkin; and whoever had that napkin could say to it, "Napkin, spread yourself out and furnish me dainty food"; and the napkin would immediately have an excellent dinner arrayed on it. The little girl handed the napkin to the princess, and said, "Your journey is so hard and lonely you need the napkin more than I do."

The princess thanked her and took the napkin, and went on. She came to a mountain the next day, and it was as steep as a wall, so she could not climb it. Close to the base of the mountain was a hut. The door was open, and the princess looked in and saw a woman busy about her household tasks.

"Have you seen King Valmon, the white bear, pass this way?" the princess asked.

"Yes," the woman replied, "he went up this mountain three days ago. But you can see for yourself how steep the mountain is, and how impossible it would be to follow him."

The woman had a numerous family of small children, and the children hung about her skirts and cried for food. She had in her hands a pot full of round pebbles which she now put on the fire, and said to the children, "The potatoes will soon be ready."

Then she turned to the princess and said: "We are so poor that we have neither proper food nor sufficient clothing, and we are always hungry and ragged. It goes to my heart to hear the children constantly crying for something to eat. So I have put the pot full of stones on the fire and told them the potatoes will soon be ready. That will quiet them for a while."

"Perhaps I can give them something better than boiled stones," the princess said, and she got out her napkin and flask.

With the help of these she furnished a feast to which they all sat down in great happiness. When the children had eaten and drunk as much as they wanted the princess cut them out some clothes with her golden scissors.

"Well," the woman said, "since you have been so kind to us it would be a shame if I did not do all in my power to assist you to climb the mountain. My husband is one of the best blacksmiths in the world. Stay here and rest till he gets home, and I will have him forge you some claws for your hands and feet that will enable you to crawl and scramble up the steep mountain-side."

As soon as the blacksmith arrived he set to work making the claws, and next morning they were ready. The princess at once put them on, and began climbing. All that day and all the following night she slowly toiled upward until she was so tired she could scarce lift hand or foot and thought she must slip and fall down the precipitous rocks. But just then she reached the top of the mountain and found herself on a broad, level plateau, and near at hand was a castle which swarmed with workmen who were as busy as ants on an ant-hill.

"What is going on here?" the princess asked.

"This is the home of an old hag who has bewitched King Valmon," they replied. "In three days she will marry him, and we are making ready for a grand wedding feast."

"Can I speak with her?" the princess questioned.

"No," they said, "that is quite impossible.

Then the princess sat down just outside of the castle, and began to clip in the air with her golden scissors, and the silks and satins flew about as thick as snowflakes.

Soon the old hag looked forth from a near window, and said: "Those scissors can do more than all the tailors in my employ. I would like to buy them."

"They are not for sale," the princess responded, "but you can have them if you will let me visit King Valmon this evening."

"Very well," the old hag said, "you have my permission and welcome."

But before the princess went to the apartment of

King Valmon the old hag gave him a sleeping draught, and he was so drowsy while the princess was with him that he could not keep his eyes open. This distressed her greatly, and she wept and wailed until the old hag came and ordered her out of the castle.

Next day she seated herself where she had sat before to clip with her scissors. This time she poured out drink from her flask, and what she poured out formed a little brook that flowed away down the slope, yet the flask did not become empty.

Presently the hag looked out of the window, and said, "I would like to buy that flask of yours."

"It is not for sale," the princess said, "but you can have it if you will let me visit King Valmon this evening."

"Very well," the old hag responded, "you have my permission and welcome."

But before the princess went to the apartment of King Valmon, the old hag gave him a sleeping draught that made him so drowsy he could not keep his eyes open; and though the princess wailed and wept while she was with him he paid no attention to her. However, a workman who was engaged on some task in a neighboring room heard her, and in the morning he said to King Valmon: "The princess who dwelt with you in your forest castle has come to try to set you free. Twice she has been allowed to spend an evening with you, but accomplished nothing because the old hag had put you to sleep with a drugged drink. Beware of the wiles of the cunning dame, or your doom is sealed."

That day the princess seated herself near the castle once more, and this time got out her magic napkin, and said, "Napkin, spread yourself and be covered with dainty food."

At once the napkin became so large and the food on it was so plentiful that hundreds of men might have eaten and been satisfied. Then the old hag looked out of the window, and said: "Maiden, that napkin of yours would save the trouble and expense of much boiling and roasting here in my castle. Will you sell it?"

"No," the princess said, "I will not sell it, but I will give it to you if you will let me spend this evening with King Valmon."

"Very well," the old hag said, "you can do so and welcome."

As usual the witch prepared a sleeping draught, but King Valmon was fully determined not to take it, and he pretended that he was already asleep. She did not trust appearances, but she took a pin and stuck it in his arm to make sure he was not attempting to deceive her. Yet in spite of the pain he did not wince or stir, and she went away confident that he would not soon waken.

But when the princess came in he greeted her joyfully, and they told each other all that had happened to them since they had parted, and devised a plan for getting rid of the old witch.

By orders of King Valmon the carpenters early next day made a trap-door on the drawbridge over which the bridal train had to pass. The hour for the wedding came, and, in accord with the custom of the country, the bride and her friends rode at the head of the procession. Before they were aware of any danger they dropped through the trap-door and they were all drowned.

Afterward King Valmon and the princess took all they could carry of the old hag's gold and goods and returned to their own land. There they were married, and for the rest of their days they lived peacefully and happily.

The Bear And The Little Old Woman

There WAS ONCE a little old woman who lived in a cottage on the edge of a forest, and one summer day she took a basket on her arm and went deep into the woods in search of wild cherries. After a time she found a tree loaded with ripe fruit and she climbed up among the branches and began to fill her basket. While she was thus engaged a bear happened along, and he looked up into the tree, and said, "Come down, old woman, that I may eat you."

"Go along with you! " she retorted. "Why should you want to eat a scrawny old creature like me? Here, I will throw you one of my shoes to gnaw on. Be satisfied with that and trouble me no more."

So she threw down one of her shoes, and the bear gnawed and gnawed at it, but the more he gnawed the hungrier he grew. At last, growling with rage, he turned his eyes upward, and said, "Come down, you old wretch, and let me eat you."

"Just wait a little longer," she said. "I want to fill my basket with cherries. Meanwhile, you can have my other shoe to gnaw." So she threw down her other shoe. But the bear found it no juicier than the first one, and he soon stopped chewing it, and waited as patiently as he could for the little old woman to descend from the tree.

When she had cherries enough she said to the bear: "Surely, you could not find much pleasure in eating me, who am only skin and bones. I invite you to go with me to my home, where I have a little boy and girl. How would they suit you?"

"They would suit me exactly," the bear replied, "and I wish you would hurry." Then down came the little old woman out of the wild cherry tree, and went home, with the bear tramping along close behind her.

They arrived at the house, and the little old woman said: "Mr. Bear, I will tell you what you must do—you must wait until the children have had a good supper, for that will make them all the fatter. I will start preparing it at once, and you can run around outside to get up a better appetite."

This sounded reasonable, and the bear went out and had a lively run in the forest. By and by he returned to the cottage and rapped at the door. "Little woman!" he called, "here I am. Now bring me the children. I am half starved."

"Oho!" the little old woman responded, "you come too late. The boy has made the door fast with its stout iron bolts, and I have just put both the children to sleep in their beds. I couldn't think of waking them, and I am too old and feeble myself to unbolt the door without help. Come some other day, won't you?"

Then the bear perceived that he had been fooled, and he walked reluctantly away with drooping snout and an empty stomach.

THE BEAR GNAWS THE OLD WOMAN'S SHOE

How Bruin Tried To Bring Reynard To Court

Reynard THE FOX had been stealing chickens, and complaint of his thieving had reached the king. The king was wroth and he declared that Reynard should be punished, and he dispatched Bruin the bear to summon the marauder to court to answer for his crimes.

Away went Bruin the next morning. He passed through a dark forest and over a high mountain and arrived at Reynard's castle. The castle gates were shut and locked, and after Bruin had knocked he sat down and called in a loud voice: "Sir Reynard, are you at home? I am Bruin, your kinsman. The king has sent me to summon you to court to answer many foul accusations made against you, and he has vowed that if you do not come your life shall be forfeited and your goods confiscated. Therefore, I advise you to return to the court with me and avoid the calamity that otherwise will fall on you."

Reynard was lying in the sun just inside of the gate. After meditating for a while on the bear's words he opened the gate and said: "Dear Uncle Bruin, you are exceedingly welcome. Pardon my slowness in responding to your knock, but I was saying my evening prayer, and devotions must not be neglected. I wonder that the king should have sent you on such a long weary journey. Your sweat and toil far exceed the value of what you can accomplish. Truly, if you had not come, I would tomorrow have been at the court of my own accord. I had intended to go thither some time ago, but of late I have abstained from eating flesh, and the strange new food of which I have partaken has made me ill."

"Alas! Dear nephew," the bear responded, "what food is it that so troubles you?"

"Why," the fox said, "it is an ordinary sort of food such as poor folk eat from necessity. In short, it is honey, and, urged by hunger, I ate too freely."

"Ha!" Bruin exclaimed, "Honey? Do you show such slight respect for that, nephew? It is food fit for the greatest monarch in the world. Give me a chance to feast on some of that honey, and I will be your servant everlastingly."

"Surely, uncle," the fox said, "you jest with me."

"Jest with you!" Bruin cried. "I never was in more serious earnest."

"Well, then," the fox responded, "I will take you where there is so much honey that ten of you would not be able to devour it at a meal. It is in the farmyard of a man named Lanfert who dwells not far away. Let us go thither at once."

The bear laughed for pleasure, and thanked the fox heartily for his kindness. They set out together and soon came in sight of Lanfert's house. This Lanfert was a stout and lusty carpenter, and a few days previous he had brought into his yard a great oak log and started to split it. He had driven in two thick wedges which had opened a wide cleft. The fox pointed to the partially split oak, and said, "Dear uncle, there is an enormous amount of honey in that tree. You have only to thrust in your head, and you can eat to your heart's content. But I beg you to be discreet in your feasting, for a surfeit is dangerous."

"Trouble not yourself on that score, Nephew Reynard," the bear said, and he hurried to the log and thrust his head deep into the cleft.

Immediately the fox knocked out the wedges and the bear was fast caught. Bruin began to whine and howl and scratch and tumble about, and the fox said mockingly, "Is the honey good, uncle? Eat not too much, I beseech you, lest it should make you sick and hinder your journey to the court." Then the fox went away toward his castle.

By this time the noise in the yard had brought Lanfert out of the house. He was greatly amazed to find a bear there in such a plight, and when he saw how securely the beast was caught, he ran and invited the neighbors to come and see the sight. The news was soon known through all the town, and every one from the children up to the old men and women who had not a tooth in their heads ran to Lanfert's yard, armed with whips, rakes, brooms, and whatever they could lay their hands on. Dame Jullock, the minister's wife, brought her distaff, for she happened to be spinning at the time.

This army put Bruin into a great fright, and when he heard the clamor of their approach he made a mighty effort and wrenched himself free, though not without much damage to his scalp and ears. The villagers were approaching from all directions, and before Bruin could determine which way to fly, Farmer Lanfert and the minister and the whole parish were assailing him with their cudgels. Even Bertolf with the wooden leg was there, and he used his cane as a weapon and pounded the bear as vigorously as any of the rest.

Presently Bruin made a sudden rush, got out of the crowd, and ran toward an adjacent river. It happened that a group of women, who had withdrawn from the fray to look on and recover their breath, stood at the edge of the river bank, and the bear in his terrified flight collided with some of them and knocked them into the water. Among these unfortunates was the parson's wife, and the parson began shouting: "Help! oh help! Dame Jullock is drowning!"

When the people heard this they paid no more attention to the bear and assisted to rescue the woman from the river. That done, the minister looked to see what had become of the bear, and found that he was swimming away as fast as he could. "Turn, villain," the preacher cried in a rage, running along the bank and brandishing a stick he had in his hand; "come back that I maybe revenged on you."

But Bruin did not care to accept that sort of an invitation. He swam with the current, and at last, when he was certain that he was beyond pursuit, he came to land, groaning, sighing, and gasping as if he was about to expire.

While all these things were happening, the fox, on his way home, stole a fat hen, threw her over his shoulder, and ran along a bypath so that no one would see him. The path took him to the river, and as he came to the edge of the bank he was saying to himself, "My fortune is as I wished it, for Bruin, the greatest enemy I had at court, is undoubtedly by this time dead."

Just then he espied Bruin on the shore below, and

changed the tenor of his remarks. "What a silly fool that Lanfert the carpenter must be," the fox grumbled, "to lose such good meat—meat that is so fat and wholesome, and that was delivered into his hand with no trouble on his part. Any other man would have been quick to take advantage of the luck he has neglected."

But he soon ceased his chiding and fretting, and in a louder voice addressed the bear. "Sir," he said scornfully, "God protect you!"

"O you foul red villain," the bear muttered, "what impudence is like to this?"

The fox went on speaking. "Did you pay Lanfert for the honey, uncle?" he said. "If you have forgotten to do so it will bring you disgrace, and rather than see you disgraced I will pay for the honey myself. It was excellent, was it not, and I know where much more can be had at the same price."

These mocking words made the bear exceedingly angry, but because he could not take revenge, he made no response and let Reynard talk on as he pleased. After a short rest Bruin plunged again into the stream and swam down and landed on the other side. Thence he made his way back to the court, meditating with grief on his misfortunes.

The king was very wroth when he saw how his

messenger had been treated, and swore to punish the fox in such a manner as would make all traitors tremble. And yet I believe that Reynard still runs free in the forest, and dwells safely in the old castle beyond the mountain.

The Bees And The Bears

There WAS A TIME when the honeybees had no stings and were as harmless as houseflies. They were just as industrious as they are now, but they had no end of trouble, for they could not defend their honey from the many creatures that loved it and stole it at every opportunity.

In vain they hid their comb among the crannies of lofty cliffs and far up in tall hollow trees. Birds with long beaks would suck out the honey, the squirrels were constantly stealing it, and, worst of all, the bears were so clever in getting it, no matter where it was hidden, that very little escaped them. Whole swarms of bees often starved in the long winter because their store of food had been plundered.

At last, when they had about given up hope that any of them could survive much longer, they heard that the great wizard Wakonda was traveling through the country. He had left his beautiful home at Spirit Lake and was making this journey to help any who were in real distress.

So the bees resolved to make known their woes to him. They sent messengers to meet him and a present of delicious honey which some of them had succeeded in keeping out of the way of their enemies. Wakonda received the messengers very graciously, enjoyed the honey, and listened with indignation to their tales of persecution.

For a time he was uncertain how to help the industrious little creatures and he asked them to return three days later, when he would announce just what he would do for them. The messengers went away greatly delighted and told the news not only to their own people but to their cousins, the wasps, hornets, and bumblebees.

On the appointed day the bees were on hand, and so were their cousins. Wakonda regarded the latter rather suspiciously, but the bees commended them to him, and he gave them all a friendly welcome. Then he made a speech and praised the bees for their industry in gathering food during the summer to eat in the long cold winter. He ended by giving them the same sort of weapons that their cousins possessed.

The bees presently flew away, and now they engaged in honey-storing more earnestly then ever. Not long afterward a couple of bears, who were roaming through the forest, saw some of the bees going in and out of a knothole in a big tree. Up climbed the bears with saucy assurance, expecting to put their paws into the hole and pull out the sweet treasure. But before they had reached their goal the bees came forth in great numbers and attacked them. The little creatures did not fly around now, in a helpless panic, as they did formerly, but at once attacked their enemies. They stung the marauders about their eyes and lips, and wherever else they could reach them with their terrible new weapons.

The bears could not comprehend this unforeseen ability of the bees to fight. They tried to climb higher, but all the time the insects returning from gathering honey increased the number of their assailants. At length the bears, howling with rage and terror, gave up their effort, scrambled back to the ground, and ran away.

Other swarms served the enemies who would rob them in the same way. They were not always equally successful in defending their honey stores, but never since has there been any danger that the bees would all perish for lack of food.

Bruin's Ride

UPON A TIME there was a farmer who drove far up on the mountain side with his sledge to get a load of leaves for stable litter to keep his cattle warm in the winter. When he got to where the leaves were plentiful he backed his sledge close up to a convenient bank and began to pitch them on to the sledge.

But in the midst of the leaves lay a bear who had curled up there to sleep through the winter. Soon he felt the man trampling about and when the man's back chanced to be turned, he made a sudden leap, and landed right on the sledge.

The horse got wind of Bruin, and was so frightened he ran off down the descent toward home ten times faster than he had come up, and he carried the bear along as a passenger. Bruin was not lacking in courage, but such a ride made him anxious, to say the least. There he sat holding on as well as he could, looking timidly this way and that as he sped along in the hope that he might see some place where he could throw himself off with safety. However, he dared not risk a tumble.

When he had gone some distance he met a peddler, who said: "Surely, that is the sheriff. Whither can he be going? He must be journeying far and have little time to spare, he drives so fast."

As for Bruin, he spoke never a word. He had all he could do to hold on.

A little farther along he met a beggar woman, who said, "Ha! that is the parson." She curtsied and begged for a penny in God's name. But Bruin said never a word and gave all his energy to sticking fast, while he continued his wild flight.

Shortly afterward he met Reynard the fox. "Ho, ho!" Reynard exclaimed, "Here is Bruin out taking a ride!" Then he shouted, "Stop a moment, and let me ride with you." But Bruin made no reply, He simply held on like grim death while the horse ran as fast as he could lay hoofs to the ground.

"Alright!" Reynard screamed, "If you won't take me with you, I tell you that although you now travel as if you were a gentleman in your furs, I don't doubt that you'll come to some bad end for driving so like a daredevil."

But Bruin heard none of Reynard's ill-natured remarks. The horse galloped on until he got to the farm, and without slackening his mad pace dashed into the open stable door. The result was that his harness was torn off, the sledge came to a sudden stop, and Bruin was thrown against the side of the stable and killed.

All this time the man who owned the sledge knew nothing of what had happened. He continued to pitch forkful after forkful of leaves down the bank; but when he thought he had enough and went to tie the leaves on the sledge, to prevent them from slipping off on the journey home, he could find neither sledge nor horse. So he hurried along the road hoping that the horse had only strayed quietly a little way in search of food.

After a while he met the peddler. "Have you seen my horse and sledge?" he asked.

"No," the peddler replied, "but I met the sheriff not long ago, and he drove so fast I feel sure he was hastening to arrest some criminal."

The man went on and soon met the beggar woman. "Have you seen my horse and sledge?" he asked.

"No," the beggar woman answered, "but I met the parson down yonder. He must have some important errand; else he would not have driven so fast. I noticed that he had a borrowed horse."

The man went on and presently met the fox. "Have you seen my horse and sledge? " he questioned.

"Yes, I have," the fox said, "and my neighbor Bruin was riding on the sledge and going as if he was running away with stolen property."

"The rascal!" the farmer exclaimed, "perdition take him! He'll ruin the horse with his wild driving."

"If he does that," the fox said, "I advise you to kill him, take off his skin, and roast him in your fireplace. But don't forget that you are indebted to me for the information I have given you. If your horse comes out alright I think you ought to reward me by driving back here with your sledge and giving me a lift over the mountain. I have a fancy to see how it feels to ride instead of going on foot."

"Well," the man said, "I'll consider it. Meet me at this spot tomorrow morning." He was sure, however, that Reynard was designing to play off some of his tricks on him, and when he returned to meet the sly fox the next day he carried a loaded gun on his sledge. Instead of getting a ride, Reynard got a charge of shot that ended his life. So the farmer secured both a bear skin and a fox skin.

THE BEGGAR WOMAN ASKS FOR A PENNY

THE BEAR AND THE TAILOR

Once UPON A TIME there was an exceedingly proud princess who asked a riddle of every suitor for her hand. She announced publicly that all comers were welcome to try their skill, and that whoever could solve her riddle should be her husband. But for a long time every man who presented himself failed to answer rightly, and was sent away with scorn and derision.

It so happened that three tailors, who were traveling together, came to the royal city, and they soon heard all about the proud princess and her riddle, and were disposed to try their luck at winning her. The older two were confident they would be successful because they had made so many fine and strong stitches with never a wrong one. Surely, they could not fail to do the right thing here, too. The third tailor was a lazy young scamp who did not even understand his own trade, but he thought that luck would befriend him, just this once, for if it did not, what was to become of him?

The two others said to him: "You had better keep away. You'll never succeed with your small allowance of brains."

But the youth was not to be daunted, and said he had set his mind on solving the riddle and meant to shift for himself. So he marched off as if the whole world belonged to him.

The three tailors presented themselves before the princess and told her they had come to guess her riddle. Then, with a low bow, the two elder tailors said, "Here, at last, are the right men, each with an understanding so fine you could almost thread a needle with it."

"Well," the princess responded, "you notice that my hair is draped so you cannot see it, but I would have you know that it is of two different colors, and you must tell me what those colors are. That is my riddle."

"Your question is more easily answered than I expected," the oldest tailor said. "No doubt your hair is black and white like the cloth we call pepper and salt."

"Wrong," the princess announced.

"If your hair is not black and white," the second tailor said, "I am confident that it is red and brown like my father's Sunday coat."

"Wrong again," the princess said. "Now let the third speak. I see he thinks he knows all about it."

The young tailor stepped forward, bold as brass,

and said, "The princess has gold and silver hair on her head, and those are the two colors."

On hearing this, the princess turned pale and almost fainted; for the young tailor had hit the mark, and she had firmly believed that not a soul could guess her riddle. As soon as she recovered herself, she said: "Don't fancy that you have won me yet. There is something else you must do. In the stable is a bear with which you must spend the night. If I find that you are still alive when get up in the morning, you shall marry me."

She fully expected to rid herself of the tailor in this way, for the bear had never left any one alive who had once come within reach of his claws. The tailor, however, had no notion of being scared, but said cheerily, "Bravely ventured is half won."

When evening came he was taken to the stable. The bear at once sprang toward him to give him a warm welcome with his great paws. "Gently, gently," the tailor said, "I must teach you manners."

Out of his pockets he took some walnuts which he began cracking with his teeth and eating as though he had not a care in the world. This made the bear long for some nuts himself. The tailor thrust his hand into his pocket, and drew forth, not a nut, but a pebble of much the same size and shape. He gave it to the bear, who put it in his mouth, but try as he might he could not crack it. "Dear me," he said, "what a block-head I must be! I can't even crack a nut. Will you crack it for me?" he said to the tailor.

"You're a nice sort of fellow," the tailor said. "The idea of having those great jaws and not being able to crack a walnut!"

So saying, he slyly substituted a nut for the pebble and soon cracked it.

"Let me try again," the bear said. "The thing looks so easy as you do it that I think must be able to man-age it myself."

The tailor gave him the pebble again, and the bear bit and gnawed away as hard as he could, but all to no purpose.

Presently the tailor produced a fiddle from under his coat and began playing on it. The tune was so merry that the bear could not help dancing, and after he had danced for some time he was so pleased that he asked the tailor if it was easy to learn the art of fid-dling.

"Why, it's like child's play," the tailor said. "Look here; you press the strings with the fingers of the left hand, and draw the bow across the strings with the right hand, so. Then the tune goes up and down—tra-la-la-la-la!"

"Oh!" the bear cried, "I wish I could play like that. Then I could dance whenever I felt disposed to do so.

Will you give me some lessons?"

"Certainly," the tailor said, "if you will do your best to learn. But let me look at your paws. Dear me! Your nails are terribly long. I must cut them before you can handle a fiddle."

In a corner of the stable was a wooden vise and he had the bear put his paws in it, and screwed them fast. "Now wait while I fetch my scissors," he said, and he lay down in a corner and went to sleep.

The bear was very uncomfortable, and he groaned and growled so loudly that he was heard by the princess in her room in the palace. She thought he was roaring with delight as he destroyed the tailor. Next morning she rose feeling quite cheerful and free from care, but when she glanced out toward the stable there stood the tailor in front of the door looking as fresh and lively as a fish in the water. She was much disturbed, but her promise to marry him had been made publicly, and the promise could not be broken without disgracing her. So the king ordered out the state coach to take her and the tailor to church to be married.

As they were starting, the other two tailors, who were envious of the younger one's good fortune, went to the stable and released the bear from the vise. Immediately the beast gave chase to the carriage, foaming at the mouth with rage. The princess heard him coming, puffing and growling, and she was much frightened. "Oh dear!" she cried, "the bear is after us!"

But the tailor was not alarmed in the least. He stood on his head, stuck his legs out of the carriage window, and shouted to the bear: "Do you see this vise? If you don't go back this minute I'll screw you tight into it."

The bear wanted nothing more to do with a vise, and he turned round and ran off as fast as he could go, while the carriage continued its journey to the church. There the tailor and the princess were married, and he lived with her afterward many years as merry as a lark.

Whoever does not believe this story must pay a dollar.

**WIHQSH
(THE END)**